PERCY JACKSON & THE OLYMPIANS

BOOK FOUR

THE BATTLE OF THE LABYRINTH

The Graphic Novel

by

RICK RIORDAN

Adapted by
Robert Venditti

Art by
Orpheus Collar
and Antoine Dodé

Lettering by
Chris Dickey

DISNEP · HYPERION
Los Angeles New York

Adapted from the novel
Percy Jackson & the Olympians, Book Four: *The Battle of the Labyrinth*

Text copyright © 2018 by Rick Riordan
Illustrations copyright © 2018 by Disney Enterprises, Inc.

First Edition, October 2018
1 3 5 7 9 10 8 6 4 2
FAC-008598-18236
Printed in the United States of America

This book is set in Adobe Caslon Pro/Adobe;
MonsterFonts-HouseofTerror, Tiki-Island/House Industries

Layouts and Color by Orpheus Collar
Pencils and Inks by Antoine Dodé
Designed by Jim Titus

Library of Congress Cataloging-in-Publication Data

Names: Venditti, Robert, author. • Riordan, Rick. Battle of the Labyrinth.
Title: The battle of the Labyrinth : the graphic novel / by Rick Riordan ; adapted by Robert Venditti ;
art and color by Orpheus Collar and Antoine Dode.
Description: First graphic novel edition. • Los Angeles ; New York : Disney-Hyperion, 2018. • Series:
Percy Jackson & the Olympians ; book 4 • Summary: When demonic cheerleaders invade his high school, Percy
Jackson hurries to Camp Half-Blood, from whence he and his demigod friends set out on a quest through the
Labyrinth, while the war between the Olympians and the evil Titan lord Kronos draws near.
Identifiers: LCCN 2017053599 • ISBN 9781484782354 (hardcover) • ISBN 9781484786390 (paperback)
Subjects: LCSH: Graphic novels. • CYAC: Graphic novels. • Mythology, Greek—Fiction. • Labyrinths—
Fiction. • Camps—Fiction. • Monsters—Fiction. • Animals, Mythical—Fiction. • Titans (Mythology)—
Fiction. • Riordan, Rick. Battle of the Labyrinth—Adaptations.
Classification: LCC PZ7.7.V48 Bat 2018 • DDC 741.5/973—dc23
LC record available at https://lccn.loc.gov/2017053599

ISBN (hardcover) 978-1-4847-8235-4
ISBN (paperback) 978-1-4847-8639-0

Reinforced binding

Follow @ReadRiordan and visit www.DisneyBooks.com

NEW YORK CITY.

NINTH GRADE ORIENTATION DAY.

GYMNASIUM

RUN!

LET ME GO!

AAAAIIIEEE!

NO!

FOOOMP!

YOU KILLED MY TRAINEE! SHE WAS GOING TO BE A GOOD EMPOUSA, LIKE ME. SERVANTS OF **HECATE** FORMED US FROM ANIMAL, BRONZE, AND GHOST.

YOU'LL **PAY,** PERCY JACKSON. SOON, YOUR PRETTY LITTLE CAMP WILL BE IN FLAMES.

YOUR FRIENDS WILL BE SLAVES TO THE LORD OF TIME.

I WILL BE MERCIFUL. I WILL END YOUR LIFE NOW, BEFORE YOU HAVE TO WITNESS ANY OF IT.

KRAKOOOM

RACHEL?

YEAH?

WINDOW.

GO!

SO, LIKE, ARE YOU GOING TO ALMOST GET ME KILLED *EVERY* TIME I SEE YOU?

POSSIBLY.

WELCOME TO *MY* WORLD.

THOSE *KILLER CHEERLEADERS* DIDN'T WANT ME.

THEY'RE AFTER YOU.

YOU'D BETTER GET GOING.

MY PHONE NUMBER. I WANT TO KNOW MORE ABOUT HALF-BLOODS. AND GODS AND MONSTERS.

YOU *WILL* CALL ME.

YOU OWE ME THAT MUCH.

WAIT! DO YOU EVEN HAVE A *SAFE PLACE* TO GO?

A *SAFE PLACE*?

SOUNDS LIKE YOUR SUMMER STARTED WITH A *BANG,* SEAWEED BRAIN.

DON'T YOU USUALLY WAIT FOR A SCHOOL YEAR TO *START* BEFORE YOU DESTROY EVERYTHING?

ORIENTATION DAY HAS TO BE SOME KIND OF *HALF-BLOOD RECORD.*

YOU SOUND LIKE MY *MOM.*

SHE'S TAKING THIS ONE A LITTLE HARD, GOODE BEING WHERE HER BOYFRIEND, PAUL, TEACHES AND ALL.

HOW ABOUT YOU, ANNABETH?

HOW WAS EIGHTH GRADE?

MONSTER-INFESTED. THINGS ARE DEFINITELY GETTING *WORSE* OUT THERE.

IT'S GOOD TO BE BACK AT CAMP, I'LL SAY THAT.

ANY WORD ON *LUKE?*

MOUNT TAM IS STILL OVERRUN WITH MONSTERS.

I HAVEN'T BEEN BACK SINCE WE FOUGHT LUKE THERE LAST SUMMER.

BUT I DON'T THINK HE'S UP THERE. I THINK I'D KNOW IF HE WAS.

ANYWAY, YOU'VE GOT LOTS OF CATCHING UP TO DO.

COME ON.

"YOU NEED TO MEET THE NEW INSTRUCTOR."

MRS. O'LEARY! DOWN!

DON'T WORRY ABOUT HER, PERCY.

SHE'S HARMLESS, AS FAR AS HELLHOUNDS GO.

TRIPLE G RANCH THIS END UP.

HARMLESS. RIGHT.

GRRRRRR

SHLORRRP

I'M QUINTUS. I'M HELPING OUT AT CAMP WHILE MR. D IS AWAY SHORING UP ALLIANCES.

AND YOU MUST BE PERCY JACKSON. ANNABETH HAS TOLD ME ALL ABOUT YOU.

I HEAR YOU'RE HANDY WITH A SWORD. I BELIEVE I'D LIKE TO SEE THAT.

TRIPLE G RANCH THIS END UP.

WHAT'S IN THE CRATES, QUINTUS?

BAROOOOOOO

THERE'S THE HORN FOR DINNER. YOU TWO BETTER GET MOVING.

THE DINING PAVILION.

BROTHER! YOU'RE HERE!

NOW WE CAN EAT PEANUT BUTTER SANDWICHES AND RIDE *FISH PONIES* AND MAKE MONSTERS GO *BOOM!*

TYSON!

OW, WATCH THE RIBS. THE *RIBS*.

GROVER? NO SMILES? YOU'RE SEEING YOUR *BEST FRIEND* FOR THE FIRST TIME SINCE LAST SUMMER.

I'M SORRY, PERCY. IT'S JUST...

THE FAT *SATYR BOSSES* SAY GROVER IS A *LIAR*.

I TOLD THE *COUNCIL OF CLOVEN ELDERS* HOW I HEARD THE VOICE OF THE NATURE GOD *PAN* SPEAK TO ME DURING OUR QUEST LAST SUMMER, BUT THEY DON'T BELIEVE ME.

THEY SAID I ONLY HAVE ONE WEEK LEFT TO FIND PAN, OR THEY'RE GOING TO REVOKE MY *SEARCHER'S LICENSE* FOR GOOD.

I'LL BE A *DISGRACE* TO THE UNDERWOOD NAME.

MY DAD WAS A SEARCHER. MY GRANDFATHER WAS A SEARCHER...

"--PERCY JACKSON."

PERCY?

HM?

ARE YOU ALL RIGHT? DID YOU LISTEN TO ANYTHING I SAID?

YEAH, SORRY. I GUESS I'M JUST TIRED.

IT'S BEEN A LONG DAY FULL OF *HELLHOUNDS* AND *EXPLODING CHEERLEADERS.*

WELL, *SNAP* OUT OF IT.

WE HAVE TO MEET WITH ANNABETH AND CLARISSE TO DISCUSS PLANS.

NOT TONIGHT. I WON'T BE ANY GOOD.

TOMORROW, OKAY?

OKAY...

THE NEXT MORNING.

KNOCK KNOCK

≥YAWN≤

ALL RIGHT! *ALL RIGHT!*

CHIRON? WHAT'S GOING ON?

I'LL LEAVE YOU TO DISCUSS THAT WITH YOUR FRIENDS.

WHERE'S TYSON?

HE LEFT EARLY FOR WEAPONS-FORGING CLASS. WHAT'S THIS ABOUT?

IT'S ABOUT THE *LABYRINTH.*

⸮GROAN⸮

LOOK, GROVER IS IN TROUBLE. THERE'S ONLY *ONE WAY* I CAN FIGURE TO HELP HIM. IT'S THE LABYRINTH. THAT'S WHAT CLARISSE AND I HAVE BEEN UP TO.

YOU MEAN THE MAZE FROM ANCIENT GREEK MYTHOLOGY? THE PLACE WHERE THEY KEPT THE MINOTAUR?

EXACTLY. IT MOVED TO THE UNITED STATES WITH THE HEART OF WESTERN CIVILIZATION, JUST LIKE MOUNT OLYMPUS BEING ABOVE THE EMPIRE STATE BUILDING.

EXCEPT THE LABYRINTH IS *HUGE*. IT KEPT GROWING OVER THE MILLENNIA. IT WOULDN'T FIT UNDER A SINGLE *CITY* ANYMORE, MUCH LESS A BUILDING.

SUPPOSEDLY, YOU CAN GET ANYWHERE THROUGH THE LABYRINTH. IF YOU DON'T GET *LOST*. OR DIE A *HORRIBLE DEATH*.

THERE HAS TO BE A WAY. CLARISSE SURVIVED, SO DID CHRIS.

HE ONLY GOT DRIVEN *INSANE*. THAT'S MUCH BETTER.

HOLD UP. WHO'S INSANE?

REMEMBER CHRIS RODRIGUEZ FROM THE HERMES CABIN? HE SWITCHED SIDES AND JOINED UP WITH LUKE.

CLARISSE FOUND HIM WANDERING THE *DESERT* IN ARIZONA LAST SUMMER, BABBLING ABOUT "*STRING*." AND HE SAID LUKE'S FORCES HAVE BEEN EXPLORING THE LABYRINTH.

AND...

YOU'RE *HOPELESS*, SEAWEED BRAIN.

THANK THE GODS *ONE* OF US IS A CHILD OF THE GODDESS OF WISDOM AND BATTLE STRATEGY.

COME ON, GRAB YOUR STUFF. WE'LL TALK MORE IN THE WOODS.

WHY ARE WE GOING TO THE WOODS?

QUINTUS ANNOUNCED *WAR GAMES*. YOU AND I HAVE BEEN PARTNERED UP.

"YOU COULD *DEFINITELY* USE THE TRAINING."

YOU ALL KNOW YOUR TWO-PERSON TEAMS.

YOUR GOAL IS SIMPLE: COLLECT THE *GOLD LAURELS* WITHOUT DYING.

THERE ARE SIX MONSTERS. EACH HAS A SILK PACKAGE TIED TO ITS BACK, BUT ONLY ONE HOLDS THE PRIZE.

YOU MUST FIND THE WREATH BEFORE THE OTHER TEAMS.

AND, OF COURSE, YOU'LL HAVE TO *SLAY* THE MONSTERS TO GET IT.

LET *THE GAMES BEGIN!*

YOU THINK GROVER AND TYSON WILL BE ALL RIGHT?

THEY'LL BE FINE. COME ON.

LET'S WORRY ABOUT HOW WE'RE GOING TO STAY *ALIVE.*

THE WOODS.

SO...*STRING*. WHAT DO YOU THINK CHRIS RODRIGUEZ WAS TALKING ABOUT?

IT HAS TO BE *ARIADNE'S STRING*. IT'S A MAGIC ITEM THAT HELPED THESEUS ESCAPE THE LABYRINTH IN THE OLD DAYS.

IF LUKE FINDS IT, HE'LL BE ABLE TO NAVIGATE THE LABYRINTH, MOVE HIS ARMY AROUND IN SECRET, AND *AMBUSH* ANYWHERE, ANYTIME.

MAYBE EVEN WITHIN THE BORDERS OF CAMP.

THE CLOSEST ENTRANCE CLARISSE FOUND WAS IN MANHATTAN. BUT THAT DOESN'T MEAN THERE AREN'T OTHERS.

ANNABETH... I HAD A VISION. I SAW *NICO DI ANGELO*. I THINK HE WAS IN THE UNDERWORLD. HE WAS WITH A GHOST. THEY'RE PLOTTING REVENGE AGAINST ME.

THE GHOST SAID SOMETHING ABOUT A *MAZE*.

THAT SETTLES IT. WE *HAVE* TO FIGURE OUT THE LABYRINTH.

WHATEVER COMES OUT OF THOSE BUSHES, I'LL DRAW ITS ATTENTION FORWARD. USE YOUR MAGIC HAT TO TURN INVISIBLE AND SNEAK AROUND BEHIND IT.

UM, PERCY?

RS-STL RS-STL

SHH! SOMETHING'S COMING!

THIS IS CRAZY. WHAT WERE WE GONE, *FIVE MINUTES*? HOW IS IT NIGHT? WHAT HAPPENED TO THE SCORPIONS?

WE FOUND IT. I CAN'T BELIEVE WE FOUND IT.

WHAT, ANNABETH? *WHAT* DID WE FIND?

AN *INVASION ROUTE* STRAIGHT INTO THE HEART OF CAMP.

WE FOUND AN *ENTRANCE* TO THE *LABYRINTH.*

EXACTLY, CLARISSE, DAEDALUS IS THE GREATEST ARCHITECT AND INVENTOR OF ALL TIME. HE *BUILT* THE LABYRINTH. IF LUKE CONVINCES DAEDALUS TO HELP HIM, HE WON'T HAVE TO WORRY ABOUT TRAPS OR GETTING LOST.

HE COULD TAKE HIS ARMY ANYWHERE. FIRST TO CAMP TO DESTROY US. AND THEN... *OLYMPUS*.

DAEDALUS LIVED, WHAT, *THREE THOUSAND* YEARS AGO? ISN'T HE DEAD?

NO ONE KNOWS, QUINTUS. THERE ARE MANY *DISTURBING* RUMORS ABOUT DAEDALUS.

IF HE DISAPPEARED BACK INTO THE LABYRINTH, HE MAY YET BE ALIVE.

TIME IS SAID TO WORK *DIFFERENTLY* DOWN THERE.

WE HAVE TO FIND DAEDALUS FIRST. IF HE'S ALIVE, WE CONVINCE HIM TO HELP *US*, NOT LUKE.

AND IF ARIADNE'S STRING STILL EXISTS, WE MAKE SURE IT *NEVER* FALLS INTO LUKE'S HANDS.

WE NEED A *QUEST*. AND WE ALL KNOW WHO SHOULD LEAD IT.

ANNABETH.

NO WAY! THE PLACE IS A *DEATH TRAP!*

I'M OUR BEST CHANCE, PERCY. I'VE STUDIED THE LABYRINTH.

IN *BOOKS!* IT'S *NOT* THE SAME THING!

ENOUGH.

I DO NOT RELISH THE THOUGHT, BUT ANNABETH IS *BEST QUALIFIED* FOR THIS QUEST.

IF THERE ARE NO OBJECTIONS?

VERY WELL.

ANNABETH, IT'S YOUR TIME TO VISIT THE *ORACLE*. THEN WE SHALL DISCUSS WHAT TO DO NEXT.

"ASSUMING YOU RETURN TO US IN ONE PIECE."

YOU SHALL DELVE IN THE DARKNESSS OF THE ENDLESSS MAZE.

THE DEAD, THE TRAITOR, AND THE LOSSST ONE RAISE.

YOU SHALL RISE OR FALL BY THE GHOSSST KING'S HAND, THE CHILD OF ATHENA'S FINAL SSSTAND.

DESSSTROY WITH A HERO'S FINAL BREATH.

AND LOSE A LOVE TO WORSE THAN....

...

YES? AND?

ANNABETH? YOU OKAY?

I'VE WANTED TO LEAD A QUEST SINCE I WAS SEVEN.

I'M WORRIED, PERCY.

MAYBE I SHOULDN'T HAVE ASKED YOU TO DO THIS. OR TYSON AND GROVER.

HEY, IT'S... IT'S OKAY. WE'VE HAD PLENTY OF PROBLEMS BEFORE, AND WE SOLVED THEM.

THIS IS *DIFFERENT*. I'M BREAKING THE RULES. BUT I DON'T KNOW WHAT ELSE TO DO. I NEED YOU THREE. IT JUST FEELS RIGHT.

I'VE NEVER SEEN YOU SO SCARED.

IS THIS ABOUT THE *PROPHECY*? THE LAST LINE-- ABOUT A HERO'S LAST BREATH...

IS THERE ANOTHER LINE YOU'RE NOT TELLING US? THEY USUALLY RHYME. DOES IT END IN THE WORD...*DEATH*?

GO GET READY FOR THE QUEST, PERCY.

I'LL SEE YOU IN THE MORNING.

"HE COMES TO FIND THE **SOURCE** OF YOUR **POWER**."

PERCY? ARE YOU ALL RIGHT?

...I'M FINE. STILL SHAKING OFF LAST NIGHT'S **BAD DREAMS**.

THE LABYRINTH WAS DESIGNED TO GET INSIDE YOUR HEAD.

I DON'T LIKE THE IDEA OF ANY OF YOU GOING DOWN THERE.

IT EXISTS TO FOOL YOU. TO DISTRACT YOU.

THAT'S **DANGEROUS** FOR HALF-BLOODS.

KEEP YOUR MIND ON WHAT MATTERS MOST. IF YOU CAN DO THAT, YOU MIGHT FIND THE WAY.

HERE, I WANTED TO GIVE YOU SOMETHING.

A **DOG** WHISTLE?

IT'S...IT'S **FREEZING**.

IT'S MADE FROM **STYGIAN ICE** FROM THE RIVER STYX. VERY DELICATE. IT WON'T MELT, BUT IT'LL **SHATTER** WHEN YOU BLOW IT. SO ONLY USE IT WHEN YOU REALLY NEED HELP.

USE IT FOR WHAT?

THERE IS NO MORE TIME TO DELAY. WE WILL ERECT DEFENSES HERE AS BEST WE CAN.

BUT I NEED NOT REMIND YOU THAT IT IS MUCH MORE PREFERABLE THAT LUKE'S ATTACK **NEVER** COMES.

I OFFER ONE LAST WORD OF CAUTION: IT MAY NOT BE ONLY NAVIGATION THAT OUR ENEMIES SEEK.

THEY HAVE THE PIECES OF THE TITAN LORD KRONOS, TAKEN FROM TARTARUS ITSELF.

TO RESURRECT HIM FULLY, HE WILL NEED A **NEW FORM**.

DAEDALUS IS HISTORY'S GREATEST *INVENTOR*. HE CREATED THE LABYRINTH, BUT ALSO SO MUCH MORE. AUTOMATONS, THINKING MACHINES...

...KRONOS MAY WISH FOR DAEDALUS TO CRAFT HIM A *BODY*.

WE'LL GET TO HIM FIRST, CHIRON. OR DIE TRYING.

PRECISELY WHAT CONCERNS ME.

MAY THE GODS BE WITH YOU.

YOU READY?

AS I'LL EVER BE.

GOOD-BYE SUNSHINE.

HELLO, *ROCKS*.

WHY ARE YOU HELPING US?

I DIDN'T THINK YOU LIKED HEROES. YOU TRIED TO KILL HERCULES, LIKE, *LOTS* OF TIMES.

WATER UNDER THE BRIDGE, MY DEAR. BESIDES, HE WAS ONE OF MY LOVING HUSBAND'S CHILDREN BY *ANOTHER* WOMAN. MY PATIENCE WORE THIN.

BUT I'M THE GODDESS OF *MARRIAGE.* I'M USED TO PERSEVERANCE. YOU HAVE TO RISE ABOVE THE SQUABBLING AND CHAOS, AND KEEP BELIEVING.

AND ZEUS KNOWS I ONLY WANT TO KEEP MY FAMILY, THE OLYMPIANS, TOGETHER. HE DOESN'T ALLOW ME TO INTERFERE IN QUESTS MUCH, I'M AFRAID, BUT ON OCCASION HE ALLOWS ME TO GRANT A SINGLE WISH.

BEFORE YOU ASK IT, I'LL GIVE YOU SOME ADVICE. I KNOW YOU SEEK DAEDALUS. IF YOU WANT TO KNOW HIS FATE, I WOULD SEEK MY SON *HEPHAESTUS* AT HIS FORGE.

DAEDALUS WAS A GREAT INVENTOR. THERE HAS NEVER BEEN A MORTAL HEPHAESTUS ADMIRED MORE. IF ANYONE WOULD HAVE KEPT UP WITH DAEDALUS, IT IS HEPHAESTUS.

BUT HOW DO WE GET THERE?

THAT'S MY *WISH!*

I WANT A WAY TO *NAVIGATE* THE *LABYRINTH!*

SO BE IT. YOU WISH FOR SOMETHING, HOWEVER, THAT YOU HAVE ALREADY BEEN GIVEN.

THE MEANS ARE WITHIN YOUR GRASP.

PERCY KNOWS THE ANSWER.

...I DO?

THAT'S NOT *FAIR!* YOU'RE NOT *TELLING* US WHAT IT IS!

GETTING SOMETHING AND HAVING THE WITS TO USE IT...THOSE ARE TWO DIFFERENT THINGS. I'M SURE YOUR MOTHER *ATHENA* WOULD AGREE.

NOW, I MUST GO. ONE LAST THING, ANNABETH. SOON, YOU WILL HAVE TO MAKE A *CHOICE.* ONE BAD CHOICE CAN RUIN YOUR LIFE. IT CAN KILL YOU AND ALL YOUR FRIENDS.

WHO'S THERE? *TALK!*

THE TITANS WILL RISE AND THROW US ALL BACK INTO TARTARUS.

KAMPÊ IS BACK.

WE'RE GOING *CAMPING* NOW?

NOT "CAMPING." *KAMPÊ.* SHE WAS A JAILER FOR KRONOS.

WHEN THE TITANS RULED, SHE IMPRISONED THE CYCLOPES AND HEKATONKHEIRES-- THE HUNDRED-HANDED ONES.

LIKE *HIM.*

HEKATONKHEIRES AND CYCLOPES... FRIENDS...

BRIARES!

YOU'RE SO STRONG, YOU BREAK *MOUNTAINS!*

I AM TYSON! I WANT YOUR *AUTOGRAPH!*

"WE NEED A PLACE TO CAMP FOR THE NIGHT."

ZZZZZZ

YOU SHOULD SLEEP, TOO, PERCY.

CAN'T. YOU DOING ALL RIGHT?

SURE. FIRST DAY LEADING THE QUEST. JUST GREAT.

I WAS KIDDING MYSELF. ALL THAT PLANNING AND READING ABOUT THE LABYRINTH. I DON'T HAVE A *CLUE* WHERE WE'RE GOING.

WE NEVER HAVE A CLUE. IT ALWAYS WORKS OUT.

WHAT DID HERA MEAN WHEN SHE SAID YOU KNEW THE WAY TO GET THROUGH THE MAZE?

I DON'T KNOW. HONESTLY.

YOU WANT TO TALK ABOUT THE LAST LINE OF THE PROPHECY? OR WHAT HERA MEANT WHEN SHE SAID YOU'D HAVE TO MAKE A CHOICE?

NICO IS DOWN HERE SOMEWHERE.

HE FOUND THE LABYRINTH, THEN FOUND A PATH THAT LED DOWN EVEN FARTHER-- ALL THE WAY TO THE *UNDERWORLD*.

NOW HE'S BACK IN THE MAZE, AND HE'S COMING FOR ME.

PERCY, I HOPE YOU'RE WRONG. BECAUSE IF YOU'RE RIGHT...

YEAH.

"I GOT LUNCH ON."

TRIPLE G RANCH.

QUINTUS...

SHORT GRAY HAIR? MUSCULAR, SWORDSMAN? NEVER HEARD OF HIM.

YOUR MARK WAS ON THE CRATES AT CAMP. *QUINTUS* GOT HIS SCORPIONS FROM YOU.

WE GOT A LOT MORE THAN GIANT SCORPIONS, THOUGH. FIRE-BREATHING HORSES, HIPPALEKTRYONS. THE HERDS OF SUN COWS MAKE GREAT EATING.

YOU KNOW THE SAYING--AN *ARMY* MARCHES ON ITS STOMACH.

§ACK§ WHAT'S THAT *STENCH*?

POOP.

MY STABLES. WELL, ACTUALLY THEY BELONG TO AEGEAS. BUT I WATCH OVER THEM FOR A FEE. THAT'S WHERE WE KEEP THE PRIZE *FLESH-EATING* HORSES.

THEY'RE A LITTLE...MESSY. BUT WHAT DOES AN ARMY CARE?

PLUS, YOU'RE TOO *CHEAP* TO HIRE SOMEONE TO CLEAN UP AFTER THEM.

YOU SEE, NICO, *LUKE* IS OFFERING VERY GOOD MONEY FOR HALF-BLOODS. ESPECIALLY *POWERFUL* ONES.

I'M SURE WHEN HE LEARNS YOU'RE THE SON OF HADES, HE'LL PAY VERY, *VERY* WELL INDEED.

YOU *FIEND!*

AS FOR THE REST OF YOU, DON'T WORRY. I'VE BEEN PAID WELL TO GIVE YOUR QUEST SAFE PASSAGE.

WE AREN'T LEAVING WITHOUT NICO.

IF YOU'RE SMART, THAT'S *EXACTLY* WHAT YOU'LL DO.

YOU SAID YOU'RE A BUSINESSMAN, GERYON. SO LET'S MAKE A *DEAL.*

IF I CAN CLEAN YOUR STABLES, YOU LET ALL OF US GO. *INCLUDING* NICO.

IF I FAIL, YOU CAN *SELL* US ALL TO LUKE.

NO! I DON'T WANT *YOUR* HELP, PERCY!

DEAL. YOU HAVE UNTIL SUNSET. NO LATER.

NOW RUN ALONG. I'LL KEEP YOUR FRIENDS HERE WITH ME.

PERCY, I HOPE YOU KNOW WHAT YOU'RE DOING.

ME, TOO.

I CLEANED YOUR STABLES, GERYON. WE HAD A *DEAL.*

LET MY FRIENDS GO.

I'VE BEEN THINKING ABOUT THAT.

THE PROBLEM IS, IF I LET THEM GO, I DON'T GET *PAID.*

AND IN ANY EVENT, YOU DIDN'T MAKE ME SWEAR ON THE RIVER STYX.

WHEN YOU'RE CONDUCTING BUSINESS, SONNY, YOU SHOULD *ALWAYS* GET A LEGALLY BINDING OATH.

EURYTION, THIS ONE *ANNOYS* ME. KILL HIM.

NO, DON'T THINK I WILL.

EXCUSE ME?

YOU KEEP SENDING ME TO DO YOUR DIRTY WORK. YOU PICK FIGHTS FOR NO GOOD REASON. THESE HALF-BLOODS DIDN'T DO ANYTHING TO YOU.

YOU WANT TO FIGHT THE KID?

DO IT YOURSELF.

FINE!

THANKS FOR STAYING OUT OF IT, EURYTION.

SHOOT. I'VE WORKED FOR THAT CREEP FOR THOUSANDS OF YEARS.

STARTED OUT A REGULAR HALF-BLOOD, BUT I CHOSE IMMORTALITY WHEN MY DAD, *ARES*, OFFERED IT.

WORST MISTAKE I EVER MADE. NOW I'M *STUCK* HERE AT THIS RANCH.

I CAN'T LEAVE. I CAN'T QUIT. I JUST TEND THE COWS AND FIGHT GERYON'S FIGHTS. I'M FED UP WITH IT.

TIME FOR A CHANGE, DON'T YOU THINK? ONCE GERYON RE-FORMS, MAYBE *HE'LL* BE WORKING FOR *YOU*.

NOW, *THAT* I COULD LIVE WITH.

STAY HERE UNTIL WE'RE DONE WITH OUR QUEST, NICO. YOU'LL BE SAFE.

WHAT DO *YOU* CARE IF I'M SAFE? YOU GOT MY SISTER KILLED.

IF YOU *REALLY* CARED, YOU'D HELP BRING MY SISTER *BACK!*

BIANCA WOULDN'T WANT TO BE BROUGHT BACK. NOT LIKE THAT.

YOU DIDN'T KNOW HER!

HOW DO YOU KNOW WHAT SHE'D WANT?

LET'S ASK HER.

PERCY, I DON'T THINK THAT'S A GOOD--

YOU CAN SUMMON THE *DEAD*, NICO. I'VE SEEN IT IN MY DREAMS. SO LET'S ASK BIANCA WHAT SHE WANTS.

REMEMBER. YOU *ASKED* FOR THIS.

WE HAVE TO CONTINUE OUR QUEST.

NICO, YOU COULD COME WITH US.

...I NEED TIME TO THINK.

THE BOY CAN STAY HERE AND GATHER HIS THOUGHTS AS LONG AS HE WANTS. HE'LL BE SAFE, I PROMISE.

I RECKON YOU'LL BE LOOKING FOR DAEDALUS'S WORKSHOP NOW? HEPHAESTUS COULD STEER YOU IN THE RIGHT DIRECTION.

THAT'S WHAT HERA SAID. BUT HOW DO WE FIND HIM?

I DID HEPHAESTUS A FAVOR ONCE.

A LITTLE TRICK HE WANTED TO PLAY ON MY DAD AND APHRODITE.

HE GAVE ME THIS DISK AS GRATITUDE.

SAID IF I EVER NEEDED TO FIND HIM, THE DISK WOULD LEAD ME TO HIM. BUT ONLY ONCE.

TIKKA TIKKA TIKKA

WELL? IT AIN'T GONNA WAIT FOR YOU.

I *HAVE* TO.

I WILL GO WITH GOAT BOY.

TYSON? ARE YOU *SURE*?

I WILL HELP HIM.

I HOPE YOU'RE RIGHT.

I *KNOW* I AM! TYSON! *LET'S GO!*

PERCY, GROVER HAS HIS OWN QUEST TO FULFILL. AND WE HAVE OURS.

I CAN FEEL THE HEAT COMING DOWN THE PASSAGEWAY.

THE FORGE IS *CLOSE*. WE CAN'T LET THE SPIDER GET AWAY.

IT'S JUST AHEAD...

HEPHAESTUS? WHAT HAPPENED? IS *ANNABETH*--

SHE'S FINE. *RESOURCEFUL* GIRL, THAT ONE. FOUND HER WAY BACK, TOLD ME THE WHOLE STORY.

SHE'S WORRIED SICK, YOU KNOW. EVERYONE SUSPECTS YOU'RE DEAD.

I KNOW *BETTER*, OF COURSE, BUT I WANTED TO BE SURE YOU WERE COMING BACK BEFORE I TOLD THEM.

COME BACK FROM *WHERE*?

WHAT IS THIS PLACE?

TAKE A LOOK. HER NAME IS *CALYPSO*. I KNOW BEAUTY-- I'M MARRIED TO *APHRODITE*, AFTER ALL--BUT I DARESAY CALYPSO IS MORE BEAUTIFUL.

AND KIND. AFTER YOUR LITTLE *WATER STUNT* AT MY FORGE, YOU ARRIVED HERE. YOU'D BE DEAD IF CALYPSO HADN'T LOOKED AFTER YOU.

WHY WOULD SHE DO THAT?

BECAUSE SHE MUST REMAIN IN THIS PARADISE FOREVER. *ALONE*.

UNLESS SOMEONE CHOOSES TO REMAIN WITH HER.

YOU COULD BE THAT SOMEONE. YOU'D BE SAFE HERE. FREE FROM PAIN AND WANT. A TRUE HERO'S REWARD. THERE ARE MANY *WORSE* WAYS TO SPEND ETERNITY.

LEAVE THE MORTAL WORLD TO THE MORTALS.

BUT IF YOU DECIDE TO LEAVE-- AND I DON'T SAY WHAT'S *RIGHT* OR *WRONG*--THEN I PROMISED YOU THE WAY TO DAEDALUS.

HERE'S THE THING. IT HAS NOTHING TO DO WITH *ARIADNE'S STRING.* SURE, THE STRING WORKS. THAT'S WHY THE TITANS' ARMY IS AFTER IT. BUT IT ISN'T THE BEST WAY THROUGH THE MAZE.

THESEUS HAD THE PRINCESS'S HELP. AND THE PRINCESS WAS A REGULAR MORTAL. BUT SHE WAS CLEVER. SHE COULD *SEE,* LAD.

SHE COULD SEE *VERY CLEARLY.* SO WHAT I'M SAYING IS, YOU ALREADY KNOW HOW TO NAVIGATE THE MAZE.

I DON'T...

I CAN'T BELIEVE I DIDN'T FIGURE IT OUT!

SEND ME BACK!

DON'T YOU AT LEAST WANT TO TALK TO CALYPSO FIRST? NO HARM IN WEIGHING YOUR OPTIONS.

SOMETHING TELLS ME IF I SEE HER...

...I WON'T WANT TO LEAVE.

WILL YOU TELL HER I SAID THANK YOU? AND I'M SORRY I CAN'T STAY?

I SUPPOSE IT WON'T BE TOO MUCH TROUBLE.

RUN ALONG NOW. TIME WORKS DIFFERENTLY HERE, LAD. YOU'VE ALREADY BEEN GONE *TOO LONG.* I LEFT A BOAT FOR YOU BY THE SHORE.

HELLO?
WHERE IS
EVERYBODY?

"BUT PERHAPS WE SHOULD DISCUSS YOUR TRIALS SOMEWHERE MORE *PRIVATE*."

YOU WERE GONE TWO WEEKS, PERCY.

TWO *WEEKS*?!

WHEN I HEARD THE *EXPLOSION* AT THE FORGE, I THOUGHT...

I KNOW. BUT I TALKED TO HEPHAESTUS. I FIGURED OUT HOW TO GET THROUGH THE LABYRINTH.

HE TOLD YOU THE ANSWER?

WELL, HE SORT OF TOLD ME WHAT I ALREADY KNEW. I UNDERSTAND NOW. WE NEED A *MORTAL'S* HELP.

PERCY, THAT'S *CRAZY*!

THERE IS PRECEDENT. THESEUS HAD THE HELP OF ARIADNE. *HARRIET TUBMAN*, DAUGHTER OF HERMES, USED MANY MORTALS IN HER UNDERGROUND RAILROAD.

BUT THIS IS *MY* QUEST. I NEED TO LEAD IT.

ASKING A MORTAL FOR HELP IS *WRONG*. IT'S *COWARDLY*. IT'S--

IT'S HARD TO *ADMIT* YOU NEED A MORTAL'S HELP. BUT IT'S TRUE.

YOU ARE THE *SINGLE MOST ANNOYING* PERSON I HAVE EVER MET!

SHE WILL CALM DOWN. IN THE MORNING I WILL HAVE ARGUS TAKE YOU BOTH INTO MANHATTAN. SOMETHING TELLS ME YOU ALREADY HAVE A MORTAL IN MIND.

CHIRON, WHAT ABOUT GROVER AND TYSON? HAS THERE BEEN ANY WORD FROM THEM?

I'M AFRAID NOT.

THE COUNCIL OF CLOVEN ELDERS HAS REVOKED GROVER'S SEARCHER'S LICENSE IN ABSENTIA.

IF HE RETURNS, THEY WILL FORCE HIM INTO A *SHAMEFUL* EXILE.

AND THERE IS MORE BAD NEWS: *QUINTUS* HAS DISAPPEARED.

THREE NIGHTS AGO, HE WAS SEEN SLIPPING INTO THE LABYRINTH.

HE'S A SPY FOR LUKE. HE BOUGHT HIS SCORPIONS FROM THE TRIPLE G RANCH, THE SAME PLACE THAT'S SUPPLYING LUKE'S ARMY WITH MONSTERS.

THAT *CAN'T* BE A COINCIDENCE.

SO MANY BETRAYALS. I HAD HOPED QUINTUS WOULD PROVE HIMSELF A FRIEND. IT SEEMS MY JUDGMENT WAS BAD.

BUT WE CANNOT BE DETERRED. PREPARE FOR TOMORROW MORNING. YOU AND ANNABETH STILL HAVE *MUCH* TO DO.

MORNING.

YOU LOOK BEAT. BAD DREAMS?

A MESSAGE FROM *EURYTION*. NICO LEFT THE RANCH LAST NIGHT. HE HEADED BACK INTO THE MAZE.

WHAT? EURYTION DIDN'T TRY TO STOP HIM?

NICO WAS GONE BEFORE HE WOKE UP. HE SAID HE'D HEARD NICO TALKING TO HIMSELF THE LAST COUPLE OF NIGHTS.

ONLY NOW HE THINKS NICO WAS TALKING TO THE GHOST AGAIN. *MINOS.*

NICO IS IN DANGER. I HAD THIS DREAM LAST NIGHT... I SAW *LUKE* IN THE LABYRINTH. THEY FOUND A HALF-BLOOD WANDERING ALONE.

THIS IS VERY, *VERY* BAD.

THEN IT'S A GOOD THING YOU HAVE A PLAN TO *GUIDE* US, SEAWEED BRAIN.

TIMES SQUARE.

THIS IS WHO YOU'RE TRUSTING THE FATE OF THE WORLD TO?

SHE'S AN ARTIST. THIS MUST BE SOME KIND OF PERFORMANCE ART.

RIGHT?

GOOD TIMING, PERCY. YOU CAUGHT ME GOING INTO BREAK.

MY CLASS IS DOING AN ART PROJECT TO RAISE MONEY FOR ELEMENTARY SCHOOL ART PROGRAMS.

YOU WERE PRETTY *VAGUE* ON THE PHONE. WHAT'S UP?

MY FRIEND ANNABETH AND I HAVE A PROBLEM.

PERCY THINKS WE NEED YOUR HELP. I'M NOT CONVINCED.

HELP? SURE. *NO PROBLEM.* EVERY TIME I'M AROUND YOU, *MONSTERS* ATTACK US. NOT TO MENTION, SCHOOL STILL WANTS ME TO EXPLAIN HOW THE BAND ROOM MYSTERIOUSLY *BLEW UP.*

I'M WITH ANNABELLE. I CAN'T SEE HOW I'D BE MUCH HELP.

ANNA*BETH.*

YOU CAN SEE THROUGH THE *MIST.* YOU KNEW THOSE COPS WEREN'T REALLY COPS AT THE HOOVER DAM. AND YOU KNEW THOSE GIRLS WEREN'T REALLY CHEERLEADERS.

I THINK YOU CAN *GUIDE* US.

GUIDE YOU? *WHERE?*

TELL HER, ANNABETH.

TELL HER.

FINE!

WE'RE TRYING TO NAVIGATE THE LABYRINTH FROM ANCIENT GREEK MYTH. IF YOU CAN SEE THROUGH MIST, THERE'S A CHANCE IT WON'T CONFUSE YOU AS MUCH AS IT DOES US.

BUT FIRST WE NEED TO GET YOU INSIDE. HAVE YOU SEEN ANY ENTRANCES? THEY'D HAVE THE MARK OF DAEDALUS. IT'S LIKE A GLOWING BLUE TRIANGLE.

HAVE YOU SEEN ANY? NO? GREAT.

LET'S GO, PERCY. SHE'S *USELESS*.

RACHEL?

DID YOU SAY A *BLUE TRIANGLE?*

PERCY? ANY IDEAS?

I...

IF YOU GUYS ARE WAITING FOR *ME* TO SEE A WAY OUT OF THIS, DON'T.

WHAT'S THERE TO LOSE?

FWEEEEEEEEET

WHAT, *EXACTLY*, DID YOU THINK THAT WAS GOING TO ACCOMPLISH?

SO I GAVE IT TO HIM. AND IN RETURN, KRONOS PROMISED ME THAT ONCE *HADES* IS OVERTHROWN, HE WILL SET ME OVER THE UNDERWORLD.

YOU SEE, I HAVE MY OWN PAST TO MAKE GOOD FOR. A MAN CAN MAKE A LOT OF *MISTAKES* IN TWO THOUSAND YEARS. THIS IS THE ONLY WAY I CAN BE SURE I DON'T SUFFER FOR THEM.

THAT'S YOUR BRILLIANT IDEA? TO LET LUKE *DESTROY* CAMP, *KILL* ALL THE DEMIGODS, AND THEN *ATTACK* OLYMPUS?

TO LET KRONOS BRING DOWN THE *ENTIRE WORLD* TO GET WHAT YOU WANT?

IF YOU HAD A CHANCE, I MIGHT HELP YOU. BUT YOUR CAUSE IS DOOMED, MY DEAR. THERE IS NO WAY YOU CAN HOLD BACK THE *MIGHT* OF THE TITAN LORD.

WELL SAID, OLD MAN.

LUKE'S MINIONS?

WHAT IS THE MEANING OF THIS? THIS WAS *NOT* OUR ARRANGEMENT.

THERE'S A *NEW* ARRANGEMENT. YOUR OLD EMPLOYER, MINOS, WANTED TO SEE YOU. AND HE TRADED A MOST INTERESTING *DEMIGOD* FOR THE PRIVILEGE.

A CHILD OF HADES. KRONOS WILL HAVE MANY USES FOR THIS ONE.

AND *I* WILL RULE OVER THE AFTERLIFE, DAEDALUS. I LOOK FORWARD TO SEEING *YOU* THERE.

CAMP. WE HAVE TO GET BACK THERE AND WARN THEM THAT LUKE HAS ARIADNE'S STRING.

IT WON'T BE LONG BEFORE THE *TITAN ARMY* INVADES.

IF THEY HAVEN'T INVADED ALREADY.

RACHEL, THE FASTEST WAY BACK TO CAMP IS THROUGH THE LABYRINTH.

CAN YOU FIND US ANOTHER ENTRANCE?

THERE.

THAT ABANDONED MINESHAFT.

IT'S LIT UP LIKE A *FREEWAY*.

THAT WAY.

HIDE THE WINGS, SO NO ONE FINDS THEM.

THERE'S SOMETHING ON THE GROUND. IS THAT...

GROVER'S HAT!

PERCY...

YOU ARE THE STRONGEST AND BRAVEST, GROVER. YOU HAVE BELIEVED IN ME MORE THAN ANYONE EVER HAS. THAT IS WHY *YOU* MUST BRING MY MESSAGE.

AND WHY YOU MUST RELEASE ME.

I DON'T WANT TO.

IT WILL BE ALL RIGHT. THE SPIRIT OF THE WILD MUST PASS TO ALL OF YOU NOW. YOU MUST TELL EACH ONE YOU MEET: IF YOU WOULD FIND PAN, TAKE UP PAN'S SPIRIT.

REMAKE THE WILD, A LITTLE AT A TIME, EACH IN YOUR OWN CORNER OF THE WORLD. YOU CANNOT WAIT FOR ANYONE, EVEN A GOD, TO DO THAT FOR YOU.

I'VE SPENT MY WHOLE LIFE LOOKING FOR YOU. NOW...

...I *RELEASE* YOU.

COME ON, GROVER.

"LET'S GO HOME."

MANHATTAN.

THANKS, RACHEL. WE COULDN'T HAVE DONE ANY OF THIS WITHOUT YOU. SORRY YOU CAN'T COME WITH US, BUT MORTALS AT CAMP ARE A BIG *NO-NO*.

IT'S DEFINITELY BEEN A...*UNIQUE* EXPERIENCE.

IF YOU EVER FEEL LIKE HANGING OUT WITH A MORTAL AGAIN, YOU COULD CALL ME OR SOMETHING.

UH, YEAH. SURE.

I MEAN... I'D LIKE THAT.

AHEM.

TIME TO GO.

YOU GUYS NEED ME TO CALL YOU A RIDE? MY DAD HAS A CAR SERVICE.

THANKS, BUT NO NEED.

I ALREADY ARRANGED TRANSPORTATION.

DID YOU HEAR ABOUT GROVER? THE COUNCIL OF CLOVEN ELDERS DIDN'T BELIEVE HIS STORY ABOUT PAN, SO MR. D *DISSOLVED* IT. GROVER IS LEADING THE SATYRS NOW.

IF THERE'S ANYONE READY TO PROTECT THE LAST WILD PLACES, IT'S HIM.

BRIARES WENT TO HELP POSEIDON MAKE WEAPONS IN THE UNDERSEA FORGES.

TYSON IS STAYING TO HELP AT CAMP.

THAT'S EVERYTHING THEN. THE QUEST DIDN'T GO THE WAY I PLANNED, BUT AT LEAST WE WON THE BATTLE OF THE LABYRINTH.

IT'S NOT QUITE EVERYTHING.

"DESTROY WITH A HERO'S FINAL BREATH." THE SECOND-TO-LAST LINE OF THE PROPHECY MAKES SENSE NOW. DAEDALUS HAD TO DIE TO DESTROY THE MAZE.

BUT YOU NEVER SAID WHAT THE *LAST* LINE WAS.

"AND LOSE A LOVE TO WORSE THAN DEATH."

THAT WAS THE LAST LINE, PERCY. ARE YOU HAPPY NOW?